Welcome to ALADDIN QUIX!

If you are looking for fast, fun-to-read stories with colorful characters, lots of kid-friendly humor, easy-to-follow action, entertaining story lines, and lively illustrations, then **ALADDIN QUIX** is for you!

But wait, there's more!

If you're also looking for stories with tables of contents; word lists; about-the-book questions; 64, 80, or 96 pages; short chapters; short paragraphs; and large fonts, then **ALADDIN QUIX** is *definitely* for you!

ALADDIN QUIX: The next step between ready to reads and longer, more challenging chapter books, for readers five to eight years old.

Read more ALADDIN QUIX books featuring Mack Rhino!

Book 1: *The Big Race Lace Case*

Book 2: *The Candy Caper Case*

Book 3: *The Unfair Fair Case*

MACK RHINO, PRIVATE EYE

The Lost Lost-and-Found Case

BY PAUL DUBOIS JACOBS
AND JENNIFER SWENDER

ILLUSTRATED BY
KARL WEST

ALADDIN QUIX
New York   London   Toronto   Sydney   New Delhi

For Paul V.

This book is a work of fiction. Any references to historical events, real people, or real places are used fictitiously. Other names, characters, places, and events are products of the author's imagination, and any resemblance to actual events or places or persons, living or dead, is entirely coincidental.

ALADDIN QUIX
Simon & Schuster Children's Publishing Division
1230 Avenue of the Americas, New York, New York 10020
First Aladdin QUIX hardcover edition May 2022
Text copyright © 2022 by Jennifer Swender and Paul DuBois Jacobs
Illustrations copyright © 2022 by Karl West
Also available in an Aladdin QUIX paperback edition.
All rights reserved, including the right of reproduction in whole or in part in any form.
ALADDIN and the related marks and colophon are trademarks of Simon & Schuster, Inc.
For information about special discounts for bulk purchases, please contact Simon & Schuster Special Sales at 1-866-506-1949 or business@simonandschuster.com.
The Simon & Schuster Speakers Bureau can bring authors to your live event. For more information or to book an event contact the Simon & Schuster Speakers Bureau at 1-866-248-3049 or visit our website at www.simonspeakers.com.
Designed by Tiara Iandiorio
The illustrations for this book were rendered digitally.
The text of this book was set in Archer Medium.
Manufactured in the United States of America 0322 LAK
2 4 6 8 10 9 7 5 3 1
Library of Congress Control Number 2021945992
ISBN 9781534480001 (hc)
ISBN 9781534479999 (pbk)
ISBN 9781534480018 (ebook)

Cast of Characters

Mack Rhino, Private Eye: a detective

Redd Oxpeck: Mack's trusted assistant

Mr. Penn: Principal Crane's assistant

Principal Crane: principal at Coral Cove Elementary School

Surfer Joe: a surf instructor; a Career Day guest

Lifeguard Sally: a lifeguard; a Career Day guest

Bella: a bike mechanic; a Career Day guest

Axel: Bella's child; a student at Coral Cove Elementary School

Daisy: a florist; a Career Day guest

Rose: Daisy's child; a student at Coral Cove Elementary School

Coach Jim: a PE teacher at Coral Cove Elementary School

T. J.: Terry Berry's child; a student at Coral Cove Elementary School

Terry Berry: owner of the Smoothie Shack; a Career Day guest

Contents

Chapter 1: Guest of Honor — 1

Chapter 2: Lost! — 8

Chapter 3: Spot Check — 17

Chapter 4: Digging for Clues — 25

Chapter 5: A Mystery Afoot — 34

Chapter 6: Found? — 42

Chapter 7: Going Bananas — 52

Chapter 8: Picture Perfect — 62

Word List — 70

Questions — 72

Guest of Honor

Snug in his office at Number 21 Beach Street, **Mack Rhino**, Private Eye, rolled up the blinds and rolled up his sleeves.

For cases big or small, Mack Rhino, Private Eye, was your guy.

Or... rhino.

As he did each morning, Mack poured himself a mug of chocolate milk. He took out his notebook. He reviewed his list.

> Tie √
> Magnifying glass √
> Class picture?

Now, where was that class picture? Mack lifted a big box onto his desk. The box was filled with childhood photographs.

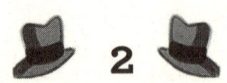

He picked up a photo. It showed a baby Mack Rhino taking his first steps. Mack smiled.

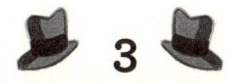

He picked up another photo. It showed a young Mack Rhino blowing out candles at his fifth birthday party. Mack smiled again.

Just then, his trusted assistant, **Redd Oxpeck**, flew in.

"Good morning, Boss," said Redd. "Are you ready to go?"

"Not quite yet, Redd. I'm still looking for our class picture," said Mack. "I wanted to share it with the students today."

Mack Rhino was this year's

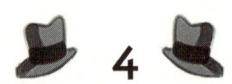

Guest of Honor at Coral Cove Elementary School's **Career** Day.

The invitation from Mack and Redd's old elementary school arrived soon after they had solved their 102nd case.

Case #102—The Unfair Fair Case—had plenty of ups and downs. **It was quite a ride!**

Good thing Mack and Redd enjoyed a little clowning around. They managed to solve the case and make some balloon animals, all at the same time.

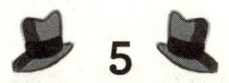

Mack reached into the box of photos. "The class picture must be here somewhere," he said.

"I can lend you a hand . . . or wing," said Redd.

But even with Redd's help, Mack could not find the class picture.

"It's probably lost," said Mack.

"You could be right," said Redd. "And we don't want to be late for school."

Mack nodded and tucked his notebook into his pocket. He picked up his magnifying glass. He straightened his tie.

"Are you ready for a walk down *memory lane*?" he asked.

Redd grabbed his camera. "I thought we were walking down Beach Street." He giggled.

Lost!

Mack and Redd hurried out the door.

They passed Bella's Bikes and Bells. They passed Daisy's Blossom Barn. They passed Terry Berry's Smoothie Shack.

In no time at all, they reached Coral Cove Elementary School. A colorful banner decorated the front entrance.

Welcome, Career Day Guests!

Mack and Redd's first stop was the main office. A busy bear sat behind a large desk.

"Good morning," said Mack.

"I'm Mack Rhino, Private Eye. And this is my trusted assistant, Redd Oxpeck."

"Nice to meet you," said the bear. "I'm **Mr. Penn**, **Principal Crane**'s new assistant."

"Sorry we're late," said Mack. "I was trying to find our old class picture."

"No worries," said Mr. Penn. "The other Career Day guests just got here. Principal Crane is in the **auditorium**. She's testing the sound system."

"Sound system?" asked Mack.

"For your Guest-of-Honor speech," said Mr. Penn.

"Speech?" asked Mack.

"Only a few words," said Mr. Penn. "The students are very excited for the Q&A."

"Q&A?" asked Mack.

"Questions and answers, Boss," Redd whispered.

"I'll try my best," said Mack.

Mack and Redd started down the hallway. Not much had changed since their student days.

They heard music coming from the band room. They heard balls bouncing in the gym.

They soon reached the lobby outside the auditorium. The other Career Day guests were busy

organizing their display tables. Mack spotted the usual faces—**Surfer Joe, Lifeguard Sally,** and many other friends from around Coral Cove.

"Mack Rhino and Redd Oxpeck!" called a voice.

It was Ms. Crane, Mack and Redd's favorite teacher. Now she was Principal Crane.

"The sound system is all ready for your speech," she said excitedly.

"My speech is *now*?" asked Mack.

"Not quite yet," she said. "First, the students will **mingle** with the Career Day guests. Then we'll move into the auditorium for your speech."

Mack gulped.

"He's a little nervous," said Redd.

"You'll be great," said Principal Crane. "And afterward, we'll all head to the **cafeteria** for a special snack."

"Yum!" said Redd. "Snack was always my favorite part of the school day."

But before Mack and Redd could start setting up their display, Mr. Penn came rushing up to them.

"We have a problem!" he said.

"What is it?" asked Principal Crane.

"The lost and found," said Mr. Penn. **"It's . . . lost!"**

"*Lost?*" squawked Redd.

"Everything has disappeared," said Mr. Penn.

"Is that so?" said Mack. "This could be the start of Case #103!"

3
Spot Check

"Thank goodness we have Mack Rhino, Private Eye, here today," said Principal Crane.

Mack took out his magnifying glass.

"I'm happy to help," said Mack.

They all followed Mr. Penn. He stopped outside the office door.

A sign on the wall read: LOST AND FOUND.

"The box was right here," said Mr. Penn. He pointed to the empty spot.

"Do you remember what was in the box?" asked Mack.

"Let me think," said Mr. Penn. "There was a winter boot, a roller skate, a bike helmet, a sun hat, and one polka-dotted sock."

"Interesting," said Mack. He took out his notebook. He jotted down the list of items.

> Boot
> Skate
> Helmet
> Hat
> Sock

Next, Mack took out his magnifying glass. He inspected the area.

On the floor, he noticed something small, round, and . . . *blue*? He picked it up.

"What is it?" asked Principal Crane.

"It appears to be a blueberry," said Mack.

"Sweet!" said Redd. **"Our first clue!"**

Mack turned to Mr. Penn. "When did you last see the lost and found?" he asked.

"It was just before eight-thirty this morning," said Mr. Penn. "After that, Principal Crane and I were busy greeting the Career Day guests."

"Do you happen to have a guest list?" asked Mack.

"Right here," said Principal Crane. She handed Mack a piece of paper.

NAME	CAREER
Bella	Bike Mechanic
Daisy	Florist
Joe	Surf Instructor
Sally	Lifeguard
Mack Rhino	Private Eye
Redd Oxpeck	Trusted Assistant

"This could be useful," said Mack. "Can I hold on to it?"

"Of course," said Principal Crane.

"We have a copy in our files," added Mr. Penn.

Mack tucked the guest list into his notebook. Then he jotted down a few questions.

> How did the lost and found disappear?
>
> Why is there a blueberry on the floor?

"Where to now, Boss?" asked Redd.

"Back to the auditorium," said Mack. "We need to **interview** the Career Day guests."

Digging for Clues

Career Day was in full swing. The students moved from table to table. They **perused** the displays. They chatted with the guests.

"Who's first, Boss?" asked Redd.

Mack took out the list. He pointed to the first name.

| Bella | Bike Mechanic |

Mack and Redd stepped up to **Bella**'s table. It was loaded with gears and seats, pedals and tools.

"Hi, Bella," said Mack.

"Hi, Mack. Hi, Redd," said Bella. "I'm looking forward to the *big* speech today."

"So is Mack." Redd giggled.

"My son, **Axel**, is excited

too," said Bella. "That's my little sprocket over there." She pointed to a student at one of the other display tables.

"Do you mind if we ask you a question?" said Mack.

"Sure thing!" said Bella. "That's why I'm here today."

"Where were you at eight-thirty this morning?" asked Mack.

"Oh, I thought you meant a question about bikes," said Bella.

"You could say we're *gearing* up for a new case," said Redd.

"Let's see," said Bella. "I signed in with Mr. Penn at the main office. I dropped Axel off at his classroom. Then I came here to set up my display."

"It looks great," said Redd. "Can I take some pictures?"

"Be my guest," said Bella.

Click! Click! Click!

"Thanks for your help," said Mack.

He looked at the next name on the list.

| Daisy | Florist |

"Let's speak with **Daisy**," said Mack.

"We're going from *pedals* to

petals!" chirped Redd with a smile.

Daisy's display table held gardening tools and plants in small clay pots.

"Good morning, Daisy," said Mack.

"Hi, Mack," said Daisy. "My daughter, **Rose**, is looking forward to your speech. She has a lot of questions for you."

"Do you mind if we ask *you* a question first?" said Mack.

"Sure," said Daisy. "That's why I'm here today."

"Where were you at eight-thirty this morning?" asked Mack.

"Why do you ask?" said Daisy.

"We're on a new case," explained Redd. He picked up a small garden **trowel**. "You could say we're *digging* for clues."

"Well," said Daisy. "I checked in at the main office. I brought Rose to her classroom. Then I came here."

"Just like Bella," said Mack. He jotted this down in his notebook.

"Can I snap some photos of your display?" asked Redd.

"Sure thing!" said Daisy.

Click! Click! Click!

"Thanks for your help," said Mack.

He scanned the lobby. More

and more students were arriving for Career Day.

Then Mack noticed somebody *leaving* Career Day. Balanced in their arms was a large box. And dangling out of the box was...

A single polka-dotted sock!

5
A Mystery Afoot

"Follow me, Redd!" said Mack. He started for the hallway.

"But what about the other interviews?" asked Redd.

"Change of plans," said Mack. "I just spotted a polka-dotted sock and it's making a getaway!"

Mack and Redd quickly walked through the crowded lobby. Then they rounded the corner and took off running.

"Walk in the halls, please!"

Mack and Redd stopped in their tracks. They would know that voice anywhere.

It was **Coach Jim**, their old PE teacher.

"If it isn't Mack Rhino and Redd Oxpeck," said Coach Jim. "Still dashing from here to there, I see."

"Sorry, Coach," said Mack.

"We're *tackling* a new case," explained Redd.

"Well, take it slow," said Coach Jim.

Mack and Redd *walked* down the hallway. But the mysterious figure with the box and the sock had disappeared.

"Drat," said Mack. "We lost them."

"Wait. What's that on the floor?" said Redd.

Mack bent down and took out his magnifying glass.

"Another *blueberry*?" he said.

"Here's one more!" said Redd.

"And another!"

"They lead to the library," said Mack. "We'd better take a look inside."

Mack and Redd carefully tiptoed into the library.

The shelves held books of all colors, shapes, and sizes. In the reading corner, Mack and Redd saw their favorite old beanbag chairs.

One jumbo. One mini.

"It sure is quiet in here," whispered Mack.

"It *is* the library," said Redd. "Besides, everyone is at Career Day."

"Let's look for clues," said Mack.

"You got it, Boss," said Redd. "I'll get the bird's-eye view."

Redd fluttered above the bookshelves.

"Do you see anything unusual?" asked Mack.

"Only a banana on the book bin," said Redd.

"**A banana?**" said Mack. "What's a banana doing on the book bin?"

"I guess it's overdue." Redd giggled.

Mack took out his notebook. He jotted down a few more questions.

> Why is there a banana on the book bin?
>
> Where is the sock?
>
> Where is the box?

"Something about this case just doesn't add up," said Mack.

"Maybe we need to go back to math class," said Redd.

"You might be right," said Mack. "Let's—"

Suddenly, there was a loud noise.

It **revved**.

It stopped.

It revved again.

"What is *that*?" asked Redd.

"Only one way to find out," said Mack. **"Follow me!"**

But before they could take one step...

Ding-dong-ding.

There was an announcement over the school loudspeaker.

"Mack Rhino and Redd Oxpeck, please report to the main office. *Immediately!*"

Found?

Principal Crane and Mr. Penn were waiting for them outside the office. A large cardboard box sat below the LOST AND FOUND sign.

"The box is back!" said Mr. Penn.

"The lost and found is . . . *found*?" asked Redd.

"Not quite," said Principal Crane. "The box is empty."

"Is that so?" said Mack. He took out his magnifying glass. He inspected the box.

Redd snapped a few photos.

Click! Click! Click!

"I don't see anything unusual, Boss," said Redd.

"Me either," said Mack. "But I do *smell* something."

Mack sniffed the air. The smell

was familiar and . . . *delicious.*

He took out his notebook. He jotted down a few more questions.

> What is that familiar smell?
>
> Who brought back the box?
>
> Why is it empty?

"I'm afraid we'll have to pick this up later," said Principal Crane, looking at her watch. "It's time for Mack's speech."

Mack felt butterflies in his stomach. "Just a few words, right?" he asked.

Principal Crane nodded.

"You'll be a smash hit, Boss!" chirped Redd.

They all hurried back to Career Day.

The lobby was now empty, but inside the auditorium, every seat was taken. The audience buzzed with excitement.

Principal Crane stepped up to the microphone.

"**Good morning!**" she said. "I'd like to thank all our Career Day guests for joining us today. And now, please welcome our Guest of Honor—Mack Rhino, Private Eye."

Mack straightened his tie. He stepped onto the stage.

"Hello, I'm Mack Rhino," he began shyly.

The crowd burst into applause.

"Gee, thanks," said Mack. He smiled. "It sure is great to be back at Coral Cove Elementary School.

I was once a student here, just like you. And this is where I met my best friend and trusted assistant, Redd Oxpeck."

"Ah, Boss," said Redd. He fluttered to the stage and perched on Mack's shoulder.

"Redd and I have solved a lot of cases over the years," Mack continued. "As private eyes, we collect clues and make **observations**. Then we put the pieces together."

One student excitedly raised a hand. It was Bella's son, Axel. "Can I ask a question?" he said.

"Of course," said Mack. "That's why we're here today."

"What was your longest case?" asked Axel.

"That's easy," said Mack. "Case #72. The Boa Constrictor Case."

"It was over twelve feet long," added Redd.

"Whoa!" said Axel. "That's like *three* of me."

"What was your smelliest case?" asked another student. It was Daisy's daughter, Rose.

"Case #39," said Mack. "The Totally Rotten Egg Case."

"We cracked that one wide

open," said Redd. "And it didn't smell pretty."

"*Egg*-cellent," said Rose.

"Hey, good one!" chirped Redd.

Coach Jim raised a hand. "Can you tell us about your newest case?" he asked.

"We're still connecting the dots," said Mack.

"The polka dots," added Redd.

"But we'll soon have it solved," said Mack. "Because I'm Mack Rhino, Private Eye. For cases big or small, I'm your guy. Or . . ."

"Rhino!" cheered the students. Mack blushed.

"Thank you, Mack," said Principal Crane. "Now, let's all move to the cafeteria for smoothies prepared by **T. J.**'s mom, **Terry Berry**."

"Perfect," Mack said to himself. He needed to think, and it just so happened that Mack Rhino, Private Eye, did his best thinking while sipping a Terry Berry smoothie.

Going Bananas

The school cafeteria was exactly as Mack remembered. There were colorful walls, big windows, and long tables.

Mack and Redd sat down. A friendly student helper soon

brought them two smoothies.

"Thank you," said Mack. He took a sip.

Yum! Banana Supreme. His favorite.

Mack took out his notebook. He reviewed his notes.

Lost box + found box + empty box = ?

This case still didn't add up.

Maybe they *did* need to go back to math class.

Mack took another sip. The smoothie tasted delicious and... *familiar.*

"Bananas!" he blurted out.

"Bananas?" asked Redd.

"The lost-and-found box smelled like bananas!" said Mack.

"Why would it smell like bananas?" asked Redd.

"Maybe your photos hold a clue," said Mack.

Redd scrolled through the photos on his camera. He paused at a picture of the empty box.

"Can you zoom in closer?" asked Mack.

Redd pressed a button.

"What is that in the corner?" Mack pointed.

"There seems to be a small hole in the box," said Redd.

"Interesting," said Mack. "Let's—"

Suddenly, there was a loud noise.

It revved.

It stopped.

It revved again.

Mack and Redd looked up. Terry Berry was busy making more smoothies. She added blueberries and bananas to her blender. Then she pressed a button.

The blender revved. And revved again.

"So *that* was the noise we heard in the library," said Redd.

"I think it's time we interviewed Terry Berry," said Mack. **"Follow me."**

Mack and Redd hurried over to Terry.

"Hi, Mack! Hi, Redd!" she said. "I hope you're enjoying the smoothies."

"Delicious as usual," said Mack. "But I do have one question for you."

"Of course," said Terry. "That's why I'm here today."

"Where were you at eight-thirty this morning?" asked Mack.

"Oh, I thought you meant a question about smoothies," said Terry. "But let's see. It was an **eventful** morning. First, my bag of ingredients split wide open. So I borrowed—"

"A box from outside the main office!" said Mack.

"How did you know?" asked Terry.

"Let's just say you dropped some **fruitful** clues." Redd giggled.

"Where did you go next?" asked Mack.

"After I brought T. J. to his classroom, I went to the auditorium to speak with Principal Crane," said Terry. "Then I stopped by the library to return a book."

"That explains the banana on the book bin," said Redd.

"A banana?" said Terry. "I must have dropped it."

"Then you unloaded the ingredients in the cafeteria," said Mack, "and returned the empty box to where you found it."

"That's right," said Terry.

"You did it, Boss!" cheered Redd. **"You solved the case!"**

"Not quite," said Mack. "Terry, where did you put the items that were *inside* the box?"

"There weren't any items inside the box," said Terry. "The box was empty."

"Empty?" asked Mack.

Did he have it all wrong?

"Oh, except for this," said Terry. And out of her back pocket she pulled a polka-dotted sock.

"I've been looking for this for

weeks," said Terry. "And to think, T. J.'s sock was in the lost and found the whole time."

"Is that so?" said Mack.

He took out his notebook and reviewed the list of missing items. He added one check.

Sock √

8
Picture Perfect

Mack and Redd returned to their seats.

"I have a hunch," said Mack. "Can we look at the photos from Bella's display table?"

"Sure thing, Boss!" said

Redd. He took out his camera and scrolled through the pictures.

Bella's table was covered with gears and seats, pedals and tools. But *under* the table, Mack noticed something out of place.

"Can you zoom in closer?" he asked.

Redd pressed a button.

"What is it?" asked Redd.

"Just as I suspected," said Mack. "A single winter boot."

He took out his notebook. He placed a check.

Boot ✓

"Now let's look at the photos from Daisy's table," said Mack.

Redd scrolled through the photos.

Mack noted gardening tools and plants. But *under* Daisy's table, he spotted something that didn't belong.

"Can you zoom in again?" he asked.

Redd pressed a button.

"A roller skate?" asked Redd.

Mack nodded. He placed another check.

> Skate √

"You were right about math class," said Mack.

"I was?" asked Redd.

"This is a simple case of addition and subtraction. Lost items were added to the box. . . ." said Mack.

"And found items were taken away!" chirped Redd.

"**Exactly!**" said Mack.

He scanned the crowd. Sure enough, Surfer Joe was holding a kid's bike helmet. Lifeguard Sally held a child's sun hat.

Mack added two more checks.

Helmet √
Hat √

Mack and Redd quickly found Principal Crane and Mr. Penn to give them the good news.

"We solved the mystery!" Mack said proudly.

"You did?" asked Principal Crane.

"It turns out the lost and found was never lost," said Redd.

"It wasn't?" asked Mr. Penn.

"Not at all," said Mack. "When the Career Day guests arrived this morning, they each passed by the box. And they each found something their child had lost."

"So everything in the lost and found has been found?" asked Principal Crane.

"Correct," said Mack.

"And I found something too,"

said Mr. Penn. "We had a copy in our files."

He held up a class picture.

"Hey, that's me," pointed Redd.

"And that's me," said Principal Crane.

"And that's me," said Mack. "For cases lost and found, I'm your guy. Or..."

"**Rhino!**" they all cheered.

Mack took out his notebook. He added one final check.

> Class Picture √

Mack smiled. He could finally **graduate** from Case #103—The Lost Lost-and-Found Case.

Coral Cove Elementary School, Ms Crane's Class

Word List

auditorium (aw•dih•TOR•ree•um): A large room with a stage

cafeteria (ka•fuh•TEER•ee•uh): A room at school for eating breakfast and lunch

career (kuh•REER): An occupation or profession

eventful (ee•VENT•full): Busy and full of activities

fruitful (FROOT•full): Helpful, useful

graduate (GRA•joo•ate): Finish school; complete your studies

interview (IN•ter•vyoo): Ask questions to get information

mingle (MING•gull): Move around in order to meet and talk to people

observations (ob•zer•VAY•shuns): Information gathered through one's senses

perused (puh•ROOZD): Looked at or studied

revved (REVD): Made an engine go faster

trowel (TROW•wool): A shovel small enough to hold in one hand

Questions

1. Why are Mack and Redd visiting their elementary school?
2. What is missing from outside the office door?
3. What do Mack and Redd observe in the library?
4. How do Redd's photos help solve the mystery? (There's more than one answer.)
5. Snack time is Redd's favorite part of the school day. What is your favorite part of the school day?